Palace in the Pond

Satpreet Bajaj

To order additional copies of this book, contact:
Xlibris
844-714-8691
www.Xlibris.com
Orders@Xlibris.com

ISBN: Softcover   978-1-6698-2047-5
         Hardcover   978-1-6698-2049-9
         EBook   978-1-6698-2048-2

Print information available on the last page

Rev. date: 04/19/2022

Palace in the Pond

It was the spring season, and flowers were blooming everywhere. Kids were on their spring break. It was a perfect time to play outdoors. Kevin and Skylar were headed to the park.

Beautiful colorful butterflies were drinking nectar from the flowers. This was an exciting time of the year.

Skylar headed toward the play area;
Kevin followed her.

When swinging on the rides, Skylar asked Kevin, "Do you like to brush your teeth?"

Kevin replied, "Not really."

Skylar said, "My mom told me a story about a prince frog who lived in a magnificent palace. He was the most brilliant frog at school and loved by everyone. He didn't like to brush as well."

Skylar continued, "Prince Frog visited the dentist and didn't get a good feedback and was suggested to brush regularly."

Kevin was staring at the bottom of the slides, and to his amazement, he saw a frog with a crown. He could not believe at what he saw. He shouted, "Prince Frog!"

Skylar was astonished at what she saw; it was indeed the prince frog waving at them.

Skylar yelped, "Price Frog is real!" As they stared at the frog, the frog ran toward the pond.

While Kevin and Skylar pushed to follow the frog,
it quickly rushed toward the pond.

Prince Frog sprinted and landed on a large green leaf, looking back at the kids.

The frog jumped into the clear pond, and they were astounded at what they found. The frog entered the most extravagant castle under water.

As the kids were looking at the palace, a large frog with a crown jumped out of the pond. He looked like the king frog. He said, "Thank you for sending my son back. We were looking for him all day." The kids were surprised to hear the frog speaking to them.

King Frog smiled and continued, "Prince Frog refused
to brush his teeth and escaped." Kevin was awestruck.

King Frog recollected, "Prince Frog never liked to brush his teeth. He would hide in different places around the palace, and this time he jumped outside the pond."

King Frog appreciated the kids and jumped back into the pond. The kids were astonished at what had happened. Skylar said, "My mom mentioned I needed to brush else King Frog would take me under water. I will brush my teeth every day."

The palace slowly disappeared from the clear pond as though it never existed.

Skylar's mom, Mrs. Smith arrived to pick up the kids. Kevin narrated the story about the king and the prince frog. Mrs. Smith replied, "It is not a real story."

Skylar added, "Mom, we did meet the prince frog like you mentioned in the story."

Mrs. Smith didn't believe what the kids said and replied, "You kids had a long day, let's get some rest," as she walked back. The kids followed her and looked back at the pond, as they knew what they saw was real.

Printed in the United States
by Baker & Taylor Publisher Services